PROMISE
NOT TO TELL

...Meagan ran, stumbling off the trail, over rocks and branches,
towards the bobbing light.

PROMISE
NOT TO TELL

by
Carolyn Polese

illustrations by Jennifer Barrett

HUMAN SCIENCES PRESS, INC.
72 FIFTH AVENUE
NEW YORK, N.Y. 10011

Acknowledgments

This book was written with the support and contributions of many people, including: Sally Cooper, Cofounder, Child Assault Prevention Program, Women Against Rape, Columbus, Ohio; Liz Calhoun, Outreach Coordinator, CAP Program, Humboldt County Rape Crisis Team, Eureka, California; Barbara Allsworth, Coordinator, Victim-Witness Assistance Program, Humboldt County District Attorney's Office; and Carolyn Travis, Sally Calligan, and Peter Lehman, my toughest readers and Meagan's best friends.

Published by Human Sciences Press
72 Fifth Avenue   New York, N.Y. 10011

Text copyright © 1985 by Carolyn Polese
Illustrations copyright © 1985 by Jennifer Barrett

Printed in the United States of America

Library of Congress Cataloging in Publication Data
Polese, Carolyn.
Promise not to tell.
Summary: While staying with her parents at a campground, an eleven-year-old girl is sexually molested by her riding instructor and learns the importance of talking about her traumatic experience with her parents.
1. Children's stories, American. [1. Child molesting—Fiction] I. Barrett, Jennifer, ill. II. Title.
PZ7.P7526Pr   1985   [Fic]   84-19767
ISBN 0-89885-239-0

For one little girl who told.

1

Meagan woke slowly from her dream of wild horses. It was her favorite dream and she held onto it as long as she could.

Then she felt the sleeping bag zipper biting into her cheek and heard Daddy, somewhere beyond the tent wall, singing *Goodbye, Old Paint* just a little off-key. The early morning campground smells of pine and cold water drifted in through the mosquito netting a few inches from her face.

Today she was going to ride a real horse again. And today, if she got to the stables early enough to help saddle up, Walt said he'd give her an extra, secret, lesson on Charlotte. Walt said that way Meagan would be sure to pass the Trail Trials on Friday.

If she did pass all the tests, Daddy promised he would rent horses on the last day of their vacation and ride with her to Crystal Pass. It was a tough, cross-country ride. But from the top of the pass they could look off into the Nevada desert. Wild horse country! If they were lucky, they might even see a real wild horse—galloping free, like in Meagan's dream.

As Daddy yodeled out the last, silly line about leaving Old Paint, Meagan sat up, threw back her head, and whinnied to him.

"Me-geee!" a baby voice giggled from the far side of the tent.

Meagan looked at the wiggling blue cocoon that held her little sister. The blue puff inched its way across the tent, then pulled itself into a lumpy ball. One fat, red curl was all of Suzette that showed.

Suzette would take forever getting up and dressed. And if she did, there was no chance of Meagan's getting to the stable early enough to help Walt saddle up.

The temptation to pull that fat, springy curl was strong. But Meagan knew that if anyone so much as looked at Suzette cross-eyed, she would scream bloody murder. Besides, if Meagan was going to get to the stable fast, the last thing she needed was one of her sister's big scenes.

So instead, Meagan stuck her head out of the tent. "Smells like sausage," she said. "I wonder who gets the extra one today?"

"I do, I do," cried Suzette, popping out of her blue cocoon. With her tangled red curls and fat cheeks, Suzette looked like a baby angel. In her arms she held an apple juice bottle with holes punched in its lid.

"You really ought to let Clifford go," said Meagan, feeling sorry for the small, brown creature that pressed its hands and long face against the glass.

"Cliffy likes me," said Suzette, rocking the bottle so fiercely in her arms that the newt banged from side to side. "I'm gonna give him my extra sausage."

2

"Well, you'd better hurry up and get dressed, then," said Meagan, pulling on her jeans and cowboy boots. "Clifford might not go for sausage," she added. "Newts like bugs. Fat, juicy, live bugs."

Meagan had guessed right. Daddy stood in front of the green camp stove at the end of the picnic table, frying sausages. He'd built a fire in the fire ring, too, and from it the battered coffee pot sent up the first weak spurts of coffee.

"Morning, Cowgirl," Daddy called out cheerfully. "Don't leave your horse in the tent. I don't want any road apples on my sleeping bag."

Meagan rolled her eyes. Daddy's jokes could get pretty gross. Still, she couldn't help smiling. You had to know how to take them, that's all.

"Sure thing, Daddy," she said, fishing around in one of the food boxes for her blue enamel cup and Suzette's yellow one. Meagan emptied a packet of cocoa mix into each cup and opened the thermos that waited for her on the picnic table. Sweet steam rose up in her face as she stirred the hot water into her cup.

"Can I help you make breakfast?" Meagan asked.

"If you'd like, you can squeeze the oranges." Daddy waved his spatula at the package of juice crystals that sat beside the food box.

"If I set the table, too, can that be instead of doing the dishes this morning?" Meagan asked. "Walt told me I could help him saddle up the horses if I got there early." She wanted to tell Daddy about the practice session, but Walt said she should keep it secret, otherwise her parents would have to pay Mr. Farnum extra.

3

Daddy scraped the crispy sausages onto a paper towel to drain. "You mean Super Cowboy's conned you kids into doing his work?"

"No, Daddy, I *want* to do it. I'm learning. Please say it's okay."

"Well, Mom made the deal with you. You'd better ask her. But remember, she just got up."

Just then Mom appeared around the corner of the Lindleys' trailer. Her hair was wet from her shower and slicked back. Even from a distance, Meagan could see that Mom's eyes were still puffy with sleep. It was the way Mom looked every morning, before going off to work.

Like Suzette, Mom was not her best in the morning, especially before she'd had her coffee. But to Meagan, Mom always looked beautiful, beautiful and strong. Now, with her plaid shirt tucked into her trim jeans, she looked like the heroine of an adventure movie.

Mom hung her wet towel on the line and gave Meagan a good morning kiss on the top of her head.

"What's this you want to ask me?" she said, her voice still a bit blurry from sleep.

Daddy handed Mom a cup of steaming coffee and she sipped it carefully as Meagan explained. When Meagan finished, Mom shook her head.

"I'm sorry, honey," she said. "You promised to do all the cleanup if we paid for riding lessons. When you make a promise, you can't back out of it just because it's inconvenient."

Meagan hesitated. She wished she could tell Mom about the secret lesson. If Mom knew how badly Meagan needed that extra practice—especially opening and shutting gates on horseback—she might let

4

her go.

"Mom, please, just this once! It might be my only chance."

"Mommy! Help me, Mommy!" Suzette stood in the doorway of the tent. She had her yellow shirt on backwards and only one leg in her overalls. "Cliffy got out. He's getting away!"

Mom sighed and rolled her eyes. "Okay, Suzette, Mommy's coming. But keep your voice down. The Lindleys are still asleep."

Then she turned to Meagan. "Please don't argue with me, Meagan, not this early in the morning. When the cleanup is done you can run to the stables. But I'm counting on you to keep your end of our bargain. A promise is a promise."

2

Just as soon as the last tin dish was wiped and the wash water poured into the drain pit, Meagan took off at a run for the pack station. Under the pines and spruce, the campground was cool, but Meagan could tell, by the spicy smell in the air, that it would be hot as soon as she was out in the open. She tore through the campground, past the trail that led to Sapphire Lake, and out onto the sunlit road.

Heat rose from the gravel and lifted her hair as she ran up the steep part of the road. The sharp granite pebbles shifted under her boots, but Meagan didn't let that slow her down.

All she could see ahead was the intense blue sky, a jumble of boulders and sagebrush, and the one twisted tree at the top of the ridge. Then she was up and over the rise, sprinting down toward the indigo lake, down toward the green velvet meadow and the first cluster of log buildings at its edge.

Farnum Stables looked deserted. Pack mules stood knee to shoulder with the fuzzy little burros in the first corral. Poor creatures, Meagan thought as she ran past. They would spend the day carrying heavy loads for the people going higher up into the mountains, but at least they would be in the wilderness. Some of them might even go over Crystal Pass and into wild horse country.

Meagan made a sharp turn around the tin-roofed barn. There was the riding ring, built of unpeeled pine poles. Across it she raced, kicking up soft, horse-smelling dust. On the far side, in the saddle horse corral, stood the horses—most of them saddled already—and Walt.

The wiry cowboy was swinging a saddle up onto Charlotte's speckled back. With a dusty plop, the saddle landed on its blanket. The muscles of Walt's back stood out under his blue plaid cowboy shirt as he leaned hard on the cinch. With one quick motion, he kneed the little piebald mare in the stomach to force the air out of her lungs.

In spite of her rush to get there, Meagan stopped short to admire Walt's skill. In one easy motion, he slipped the bridle's bit between Charlotte's huge teeth and then slid the crown piece over her ears.

"Hi," Meagan called when he was done.

Walt gave Charlotte a final, loud slap on the rump. Then he turned and tipped back his wide-brimmed hat. Sunlight lit up his blond mustache, but the rest of his face and his hands looked as dark and leathery as the dried apricots that Mom tucked in the day pack for lunch.

"Morning, girlie," he said, a grin of welcome lifting the corners of his sun-bleached mustache. The nicest thing about Walt, Meagan thought, was that he was always glad to see her.

8

Meagan slipped through the pole fence and ran to join him. "I hurried as fast as I could," she said, then looked in dismay at all the saddled horses. Only Walt's horse, Traveler, was left. And mean old Poco.

Walt tugged at one end of his mustache, his eyes still smiling. "Well, sweetheart," he said in his easy drawl, "think you can handle Poco?"

Eagerly, Meagan nodded, though inside she didn't feel so sure. On the first day of class, Poco had kicked a boy and almost broken his arm. The sorrel gelding was tall and he had a mean cast to his gray eyes.

"Now, listen," Walt said, placing a heavy rubber curry comb in her hands, "you'll do just fine if you remember two things. Don't get within kicking range of those hind legs, and don't let on you're scared. If he figures he's got you scared, he'll try and get away with murder. You got me?"

Again Meagan nodded. She wanted to ask Walt if there would be time to practice gates afterwards, but she figured she'd better get some work done, first.

Poco looked even bigger close up. Meagan walked straight up to his side and laid one hand firmly on his warm, dusty coat.

"It's okay, Poco," she told him steadily, even though she still felt a little uncertain. "I'm just going to give your back a nice scratch."

The muscles of Poco's back flickered as Meagan started raking the curry comb through his coarse hairs. Dust and horse dander sparkled in the air. Meagan gained confidence as she finished his side and legs and reached forward to ruffle loose the spots of dirt on his chest.

Now she had to move over to Poco's other side. She tried to ease her way in front of him, between

10

his chest and the rail. But Poco stepped forward. He wouldn't let her through.

"Come on, Poco," she said, slapping gently at his chest. Poco just snorted and rocked his weight forward, pressing against the raggedy bark of the fence rail.

"Get back!" she told him more firmly. But Poco wouldn't move. He outweighed her fifteen to one.

Behind her, Meagan heard Walt's amused chuckle. "That old horse thinks he's got you now."

The only other way to get around Poco was to walk past his powerful hind legs. Meagan looked at his huge, grooved hooves. Of course, she could walk way out around him; that was the safest way. But with both Walt and Poco watching her, she didn't want to act like a tenderfoot.

Meagan sucked in her breath. She walked purposefully back towards Poco's rump. Laying a firm hand on his thick hide, the way Walt had showed the class, she stepped up close, right next to his hocks, too close for him to kick her. Poco flicked an annoyed tail in her face. Meagan flinched but she managed to say "Quit it, Poco," in a firm voice. Then she was around to the other side and able to breathe freely again.

"You old creep," she said. "You just don't want to go to work today."

Poco flicked his tail at her again, but only succeeded in swatting himself.

Meagan finished the currying and was halfway through the job of smoothing Poco's ruffled up hairs with the soft brush, when she heard a voice on the other side of the railing.

"Luck-y!" It was the freckle-faced boy, Daniel, from her class. His chin rested on his folded arms and he grinned at her. Except that he was a boy, and Meagan felt a little unsure around boys, she liked him. Daniel was the one who got kicked by Poco, but he hadn't let that stop him from learning to ride.

"Can I help, too?" he asked.

Meagan smiled back at him. She was about to hand him the brush when she caught Walt's eye. He frowned at her over the top of Poco's back and slowly shook his head.

"I guess we're almost done," she said, and shrugged by way of an apology.

Now it was time to saddle Poco. Meagan lifted the matted blanket onto his back and Walt reached around her to smooth it out. Standing behind her, he helped her raise the saddle and swing it up over Poco's back. With his arms around her, Walt showed Meagan how to fasten the latigo and the girth. He stepped to one side and jabbed Poco with his knee.

"*Hoowph!*" The air burst out of the big horse's lungs and Walt tightened the girth down further. Meagan winced; it must hurt, getting kneed like that.

"Show me how you get his bridle on," Meagan said, pulling the jingling bridle down from the top of the rail.

Walt reached for Poco's head. "It's easy if you don't take any nonsense," he told her. With his toughened hands, Walt pinched Poco's mouth open and slipped in the bit.

Kids and their parents were gathering at the riding ring. Time was running out.

"What about gates?" Meagan asked. "Is there any time left for me to practice?"

Instead of answering, Walt picked her up by her waist and swung her up on Charlotte's back, even though mounting was the first thing he had taught the class.

"There you go, girlie. You lead the horses into the ring. Traveler and I'll get the gates for you." Then he laid his hand on hers. It felt rough and hot. Meagan was too startled to draw her hand out from under. Anyway, she didn't want to seem rude. He rubbed her fingers for a moment and smiled at her.

"Did you keep our little secret, sweetheart?" he asked, watching her with his gray flecked eyes.

"You mean about the extra practice?" she answered. "Sure I did."

"Good," he said, keeping his hand on hers. "I'll find some way to help you with those gates. You just trust Walt, okay?"

3

The riding class was over too soon. Before she was ready for them, Meagan saw Mom and Suzette joining the little group of onlookers near the barn side of the riding ring. Mom lifted Suzette up onto the railing between a girl with black braids and Mr. Farnum, himself.

"Meegee! Look at me!" called Suzette, waving her plump little hands.

As the line of horses walked around the ring, Meagan waved. The first part of the lesson had gone well. She'd learned how to back Charlotte between the two poles, and she'd finally gotten the knack of urging her horse forward across the plastic-lined pool that was supposed to represent a stream.

But opening the gates was something else. Every time she got Charlotte near one, the mare tossed back her head and circled away. First Walt, and then the whole class, had called out advice. "Rein her in!" "Control her head!" They all made it sound so easy. But no matter what she did, Meagan couldn't get

Charlotte close enough to the gate.

It made it worse that Mr. Farnum had watched from the sidelines. Now, as he talked with Mom, he kept looking at Meagan and frowning. Was he telling Mom what a terrible rider Meagan was?

Meagan turned away from the group of onlookers. She wasn't going to let anything spoil her favorite part of the class.

"Let's go, caballeros!" called Walt. At his signal the class urged their horses into a trot and then a canter.

Horses' hooves thudded in the dust of the ring. Around Meagan's head, the snow-capped mountains whirled. The smells of sage and dust and horse sweat filled her nostrils.

I'm the wild horse of my dreams, thought Meagan. Wild and strong and free. She tossed her head so her hair fluttered out behind her, like Charlotte's mane. If only she could gallop right out of the ring, off into the mountains, beyond the fences and trails, like a real wild horse.

The circle of riders wound down. Walt ordered them to dismount and tie up. Before the class left the ring, he reminded them that tomorrow was the last day to practice for the Trail Trials. Meagan tried to catch his eye, but Walt seemed to look everywhere except at her.

"Come on, Meagan," Mom called, holding Meagan's sneakers out towards her. "Hurry and get your shoes changed."

Meagan struggled to get into her sneakers and keep her eye on Walt at the same time. She wanted to ask him if she could get that practice in before tomorrow. If she had to go through another session of people yelling advice at her, she'd die.

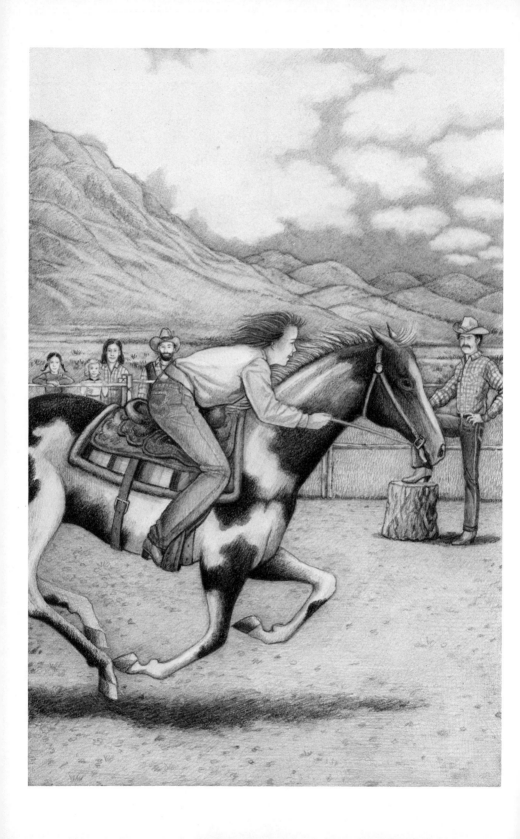

"Listen, Meagan," Mom said as Meagan yanked at her tangled laces. "There's something you should know about Charlotte and gates."

Just then Walt disappeared around the corner of the barn.

"I don't want to *hear* about it!" cried Meagan in exasperation.

Mom's disapproving silence was broken by Suzette. "Hurry up, Meegee," she urged. "We're gonna hike up to Eagle Lake and spend the whole day fishing with Daddy."

That night for dinner they had fish fresh out of Eagle Lake, the three that Daddy caught in the morning and the big speckled brown trout that Mom got just before they left. Everyone was tired from the hike and the long afternoon in the sun. Suzette fell asleep with her fork in her mouth and Mom just took off Suzette's sneakers and slipped her into her sleeping bag, overalls and all.

Meagan was tired, too, but she finished the dishes by herself, just as she'd promised.

"Better go brush your teeth," Daddy told her. "It's almost dark."

Meagan went to the clothesline and got a towel and her drawstring bag, the pink one with the horses on it. She headed for the nearby restroom. The campground was full of people, so Meagan wasn't surprised when she heard a crackling of leaves and a figure appeared suddenly in front of her in the shadowy dusk of the road. Besides, she could see, from his bowed legs and wide-brimmed hat, who it was.

"Hi, Walt," she said when he got nearer. She could hear the rustle of a paper bag. Walt was holding something under his arm.

"Hi, girlie." His voice sounded loud in the near darkness. "I brought something along for you," he said more quietly.

Meagan felt surprised and flattered. Walt hadn't forgotten her after all.

"Where's Charlotte?" she asked. "Are we going to work on gates with her now?" It was awfully late to go riding, Meagan thought, but this was her last chance to practice before class tomorrow. Maybe her parents would let her.

Walt seemed to be looking around him. Then he took a step closer to Meagan. She could smell the barn smell on his clothes and something else, a sweet, stinging smell.

"You like oatmeal cookies?" he asked, shifting his weight unsteadily.

It seemed like such a dumb thing for Walt to say that Meagan almost laughed, but she didn't want to hurt his feelings. "Nope," she said and then, in case oatmeal cookies were the present he'd brought, she added, "Well, sometimes I do."

Walt shifted the package under his arm and Meagan heard the chink of glass as well as a cellophane rustling. "We'll feed these to Charlotte, then," said Walt, taking up her hand in his big leathery one.

Meagan was going to say that she ought to ask her parents, but then Walt added, "She's right around the corner here." And Meagan thought there would be enough time to practice one or two gates if she just didn't brush her teeth. The chances of her parents saying yes to a night ride weren't that great, anyhow.

The two of them walked through the campground towards the main road. They passed families eating

18

and cleaning up and playing frisbee. In one campsite a giant R.V. sat in a pool of bright light, its generator humming, the silver glow of a T.V. screen coming through the window.

Each campsite was a separate stage, lit by its own light. Meagan could see into each scene, but behind the screen of darkness no one could see Walt and her walking on the road.

The forest was completely dark by now, and they'd gone beyond the last campsite, much farther than Walt had said. Meagan began to feel uncomfortable. She stopped and tried to pull her hand out of his.

"Let's go down this trail here," said Walt, in a quiet, gentling voice. He put his hand under her elbow and steered her down a rough dirt trail, one of the many little ones that led toward the lake.

Why was he taking her down here? There weren't any gates to practice on. Meagan listened ahead for the familiar stomp of Charlotte's hoof, the jingle of her bridle. The forest was silent. Walt stopped and set down his paper bag. Once again, Meagan tried to pull away from him.

"Take it easy, sweetheart. I'm just going to teach you something new."

Walt's hand, the one that had held her elbow, moved slowly across her chest and his other arm went around her. She felt his belt buckle press into her back between her shoulder-blades.

She stopped breathing for a moment, as much from shock as from the unexpected pressure.

Walt was hugging her.

It felt weird. She couldn't believe Walt was doing this to her.

Mom had told her never to go anywhere with

19

strangers. But Walt wasn't a stranger—he was her teacher and friend.

His arms tightened even more, and Meagan's legs began to shake.

"It's okay, sweetheart." Walt spoke in a soft, syrupy voice that Meagan hardly recognized. "We're just going to have a little fun."

But Meagan did not believe him.

From what she'd learned from her mother and from school, Meagan knew that really bad, painful things could happen. Walt was so much bigger and stronger than she, powerful and unpredictable. Like Poco. Meagan didn't want to let Walt know that she was afraid. But she had to get away from him.

"I-I-I'm cold," she said, shaking so hard that the words stuttered out of her mouth. She took a deep breath to steady her voice. "I'd better go back to camp and get my jacket."

All at once, Walt slipped his hands inside her clothes and pressed her more tightly against him. "I'll warm you up, girlie," he said in the same syrupy voice.

Meagan thought of the kind of snakes that wrap themselves around their prey and crush their life out. Her legs would not stop shaking.

In every direction, the forest was empty and dark. Meagan looked around for anything that would help her get away. Through the trees, the lights of the campground seemed to be going out. She heard the R.V.'s generator stop. The forest was strangely still.

"Let's go down into those bushes," Walt said softly.

"Wait," said Meagan, stalling for time. She couldn't let him get her any further away from camp and her parents than she already was.

"It's getting late," she said. "My parents will be worried." She didn't want Walt to know how afraid she was, but she had to make him let go of her, or at least let his hold loose enough so that she could get away. "It's dark and Daddy will be out looking for me."

Walt stopped pressing her against him. He turned to look around in the dark.

Through the trees, Meagan saw the bobbing gleam of a flashlight. "That's my Dad!" cried Meagan. "I've got to get back before he finds me here!"

As Walt's grip loosened, Meagan wriggled out of his arms and dashed for the road.

She'd almost made it when his hands caught up with her. They grabbed around her chest and pulled her back towards his body. He was squatting, so that his head was down beside her ear. His mustache hairs prickled, like an insect crawling on her neck. The stinging sweetness of his breath made her eyes water.

"Sweetheart," he hissed, "you're not scared of me, are you? I'm your friend. Don't you like me?"

Couldn't he feel her heart beating in terror against the fingers of his hands? "Yes!" she cried. "I like you!" She would have said she loved the man who beat Black Beauty, anything if he would just let go of her.

"You're not going to tell, are you?" he asked. "This is our little secret. You've got to promise not to tell."

"I won't tell," she said. But he shook her by the shoulders anyway. It didn't hurt, but it made her feel that he could crush her without thought.

"You tell, and I'll get you, good. I don't like little

girls who break promises."

"I won't!" she cried. "I promise I won't tell—I promise!"

Then he let go, and Meagan ran, stumbling off the trail, over rocks and branches, towards the bobbing light.

4

The bright light hit her eyes and blinded Meagan to everything else. She put her hands up over her face.

"Oh, hi, it's you." The boy's voice was familiar. "I thought it was a bear crashing through the woods or something."

Then the speaker laughed and turned the light on his own face so that he looked like Dracula lit from beneath. It was Daniel.

Relief flooded through Meagan. She pushed through the last few feet of underbrush on watery legs and stood on the dirt road.

"Hi, yourself," she said, trying to control the shaking in her voice.

Daniel shone the beam of light down the road. "What were you doing in the middle of the forest without a light?"

"I . . . I . . . " Meagan's throat tightened up and she found it hard to speak. Suddenly she felt very shy about what just happened. She looked down at her clothes. Could anyone tell just by looking at her what

Walt had done? She was surprised to see that her pink drawstring bag still hung from her wrist.

"Uh, did you see me?" she asked.

"No, but I sure heard you." Daniel laughed. "A moose would have made less noise. It sounded like you were running away from something."

"I was . . . I got lost and I couldn't find the trail in the dark," she said. She hoped that was all Daniel had heard. If he knew, she would feel so humiliated. Her throat tightened even more, as if she'd swallowed something the wrong way.

"I was out on the main road, looking for shooting stars," Daniel told her as they started back towards camp. "Tonight's one of the best meteor showers of the whole year."

"Uhmm," Meagan said by way of conversation, twisting the coarse string of her bag between her fingers. The end of the camp, where her parents were, seemed very far away.

It wasn't long, though, before they reached the first campsites. "Well, here's where I turn off," said Daniel, waving towards a small trailer tent.

"Wait!" said Meagan. She didn't want to be left alone in the dark, not for one minute. "I don't have a flashlight. Would you walk with me back to my camp?"

She felt so dumb asking him to walk her home. But Daniel didn't seem to mind at all. He told her how shooting stars aren't stars at all, just bits of space dust burning up as they fall to earth. Meagan only half-listened; she just wanted to reach her own camp and the safety of her parents.

"You know," Daniel said as they reached the Lindleys' trailer, "I don't understand why you have so much trouble on gates."

Meagan sucked in her breath. For a second she could almost see Walt, almost feel his hands on her body.

"I mean, okay, it's tricky, but it's not that hard. Maybe if you just reined her in tighter . . . "

The familiar glow of her family's camp lantern came into view around the dark bulk of the Lindleys' trailer. Relief welled up inside Meagan.

"Bye, thanks," she croaked, and ran by herself the rest of the way.

Meagan wanted to run straight into her mother's arms. But Mom sat at the picnic table, wedged in between the big, soft bodies of Mr. and Mrs. Lindley. As Meagan came into camp, Daddy looked up from his cards and called out: "Well, it's about time, Meagan. What happened, did you fall in?"

Mr. Lindley's big laugh boomed out at the old joke, followed by Daddy's chuckle.

Meagan stopped dead. "No . . . I . . . "

"Robert, Keith, look what you're doing to that poor girl!" The gray curls on Mrs. Lindley's head bobbed indignantly. Meagan felt grateful. Daddy's gross jokes were more than she could handle right now.

"Meagan's too old for that kind of nonsense," Mrs. Lindley went on. "She's almost a young lady. Even on a camping trip we women have to look after our faces and our hair. That takes more time than you men can imagine. Isn't that right, dear?"

It wasn't right. Mrs. Lindley was always defending people without really knowing the whole story. Still, it felt good to have her support. Now she was looking at Meagan, waiting for an answer.

Confused, Meagan nodded. The Lindleys were old friends of the family, almost like grandparents. But right now Meagan needed to be alone with Mom and Daddy.

"How long are the Lindleys going to be here?" she asked, forcing the words out past the lump that stuck like a stone in her throat.

There was a surprised silence from the four grown-ups. Then Daddy spoke.

"What kind of a thing is that to say, Meagan? The Lindleys are here to play cards with your mother and me. It's late and you should be in bed."

His face looked set, but Meagan tried again.

"I've got to talk with you and Mom, right now." Meagan struggled to keep the tears out of her voice. The last thing she wanted was to bawl like a baby in front of everyone; her dignity had already taken a big blow.

She must have been successful at hiding her desperation because when Mom set her cards down and turned towards Meagan she didn't seem to notice anything was wrong. All Mom said was, "Honey, your Daddy's right. It's late. Go get your sleep now. Whatever it is will keep until morning."

Meagan stood there. She wanted to ask if playing cards with the Lindleys was really more important than she was. She needed her parents, but the last thing she wanted was a lecture on being polite to adults.

"Go on," Daddy said firmly, picking up his cards. "Right now." As she turned to go into the dark tent alone, he added: "Sleep tight, Meagan."

Meagan crawled into her cold sleeping bag. She could hear the grown-ups' voices from the campfire and Suzette's hoarse breathing. When were Mom and Daddy coming to bed?

The tent seemed so lonely and far from the campfire. Pulling the sleeping bag over her face, Meagan hid in its cold depths. She wondered if Walt knew where her family was camped and what he had meant when he said he would get her if she told.

Her body, where Walt had touched her, suddenly felt creepy and unclean. Meagan wished she wasn't afraid to go out of the tent to the restrooms and wash up. But Walt could be anywhere out there. Maybe she should have tried harder to get Mom to listen, in spite of the Lindleys.

In the dark, Meagan rolled over on top of Mom and Daddy's air mattress. She curled up next to Suzette and waited for her parents to come to bed.

5

When she finally did sleep, Meagan dreamed that Walt came to get her. He was angry, because in her dream she had told her parents what he'd done. Walt brought his cowboys with him and they picked her up, sleeping bag and all. Meagan screamed for her parents to help her. But Daddy told her not to make such a fuss in front of the grown ups. And Mom just shook her head sadly. "You broke your promise," she said. "You promised not to tell."

In her dream, Meagan fought to get free. She twisted and clawed, but she couldn't get away because the cowboys had tied the bag up with big ropes.

The more Meagan struggled, the tighter the ropes pulled, crushing her. She couldn't breathe. Her throat ached for air.

Meagan woke, clawing her way out of the hot sleeping bag. Sun turned the tent sides golden; the warm air smelled of sleep. She was back on her side of the tent, and she was alone. Even Suzette's bag was empty.

Bolting upright, Meagan tore open the tent flap. There was Mom, feeding scrambled eggs to Suzette. Over by the car, Daddy sorted his fishing gear for the day. Everything looked so normal and safe. Meagan let out a shuddering sigh.

"Hey, here's the sleepyhead," Daddy announced. "Rip Van Winkle finally woke up."

Mom looked up from the table and smiled her pale, morning smile. "Better hurry and eat, Meagan, you don't want to be late for your lesson."

The riding class. Meagan's heart stopped. "I don't want to go," she said.

"Don't be silly," Mom answered, snatching the bread knife out of Suzette's reach. "You'll feel better after you've eaten. Besides, we're all coming to watch you."

Without thinking, Meagan pulled on her jeans and her sneakers. She tried to choke down the hard bacon and cold scrambled eggs that waited for her on her tin plate. But even the cocoa that Mom reheated over the dying coals of the fire wouldn't go down her throat.

What should she do? Meagan couldn't bear the idea of seeing Walt again. And yet, if she told . . . The terror of her nightmare washed over her.

Daddy pulled his fishing creel over his shoulder and Mom collected their swim things from the line. It was time to leave for the stables.

"Come on, slowpoke, we'll let the dishes soak just this once." Daddy came up and put his arm around her shoulder. "I'm looking forward to seeing what my girl can do."

Panic seized Meagan. She didn't want to get anywhere near Walt or his horses.

"I just want to go swimming with Mom today," she said, mumbling her words because she felt so awful inside.

"What?" said Daddy, and then it was as if he hadn't heard her at all. "Come on, Meagan. If we don't leave now, you'll be late."

"I don't want to go!" Meagan cried.

"That's ridiculous," said Daddy. "You worked hard for those lessons. What about the trail ride I promised you? How would you feel if I backed out on that?"

Meagan looked at him. Tears stung her eyes, but she didn't let them fall.

Mom came over and felt her forehead. "She's flushed. But it doesn't feel like she has a fever."

The look on Mom's face was all love and concern. Meagan felt worse than ever. If she told, she'd have to break a promise, and her parents wouldn't like that. And they'd probably be even more angry at her for going off with Walt instead of brushing her teeth. She was scared of what Walt might do to her, but she knew she shouldn't lie to her parents, either.

"I feel awful," Meagan said.

"So go riding and get it out of your system," Daddy told her. "You'll feel better once you get going."

Meagan could tell by the abrupt way he spoke that Daddy was really annoyed with her now. The horrible choking feeling rose up in her throat. "I can't."

"All right," said Daddy. "It's your choice. But Mom and I are going to think twice before we pay for riding lessons again. Do you understand, young lady?"

Mom knelt down beside Meagan. "Can you tell me what's wrong?" she asked. "Are you worried about something? Is it the gates?"

Meagan looked away from her mother's strong face. More than anything else Meagan wanted to tell her, but the stone in her throat had swollen up so big that Meagan could hardly breathe. What would Walt do? What would her parents say if she told?

"Because if it's the gates, honey . . . "

Did Mom think she was chicken, afraid of failing the Trials tomorrow? "No," Meagan cried. "It isn't the gates at all. I just don't want to go!"

"Preadolescence!" snapped Daddy as he turned away. "I guess it's started already. I still say she should go riding."

That morning Meagan stayed with her mother and sister by the lake, while Daddy went around to the other side to fish.

The sun was hot on the little white sand beach. Nearby, the water made a comfortable lapping sound. The snow-covered peaks that cradled the little lake looked close enough to touch.

Meagan had already gone swimming once in the bright, blue water, and she felt more like herself than she had at breakfast. Now, with her feet buried in the grainy white sand, Meagan helped Suzette build a little house for Clifford out of twigs. They lined the miniature log cabin with soft leaves from the bushes by the creek, so that Clifford couldn't get out. For the roof they used clumps of pine needles. While Suzette played with Clifford, Meagan dressed a couple of pine cone dolls to live in the house with him.

It was comforting to play make-believe again. The terrible dream faded in the strong mountain sunlight, and Meagan began to feel that nothing that awful had happened to her after all.

Once, when she looked over at her mother, she thought about telling her. Just so her mother would understand about this morning. And so that Meagan wouldn't have this lonely feeling inside.

Mom lay on her back, her book propped up to shade her face. All during the year, Mom worked so hard she never got to read much. Now Meagan watched as Mom thumbed through the back pages, as if measuring her chances of finishing her book in the next two days.

What would happen if I told her now? Meagan wondered. Mom would never finish her book, that's for sure. She'd probably be angry and upset. It might ruin Mom's vacation, and it would all be my fault.

In the clear mountain sunlight, what happened last night seemed almost unreal. It wasn't so terrible, anyhow, Meagan told herself. She'd just been scared. Besides, in two days they'd be back in San Luis, and she would never have to worry about Walt again.

Mom looked up and smiled at her. "Do you want something, punkin'?"

Meagan hesitated. Last night she'd felt embarrassed in front of the Lindleys. This morning she'd been too scared and confused to talk about it. Now, she just wanted things to be normal again.

Besides, she had promised. And a promise is a promise.

When Meagan shook her head, Mom went back to her reading. Using the lid of Clifford's empty bottle, Meagan scooped up mounds of wet sand and began plastering the sides of the little house. When the top was covered up it would look like an igloo, or just a lump on the beach. No one would ever know what lay inside.

6

Later that day the Lindleys said they'd watch the girls while Mom and Daddy hiked up to the top of Chocolate Mountain. Mr. Lindley let Meagan win at rummy and Mrs. Lindley asked her to help make lunch in the tiny kitchen of the trailer. Meagan knew she should have been laughing and having fun like Suzette. Instead, she felt like a snail that had crawled way up inside its shell.

After lunch, Mrs. Lindley asked Meagan and Suzette if they'd walk with her to the little grocery store by the lodge on the far side of the lake. They had to pass the stables on the way. But Meagan walked straight ahead and avoided looking toward the nickering horses.

As long as she kept her promise, Meagan told herself, she didn't have anything to be scared about. Besides, it was already Friday. By Sunday night, they'd be back in San Luis. Then she could forget about Walt, forever.

The store was a small wooden building, more like a cabin than a real store. Its outside was plain boards, weathered golden brown. The worn steps that led up to the front porch sounded gritty under Meagan's sneakers.

A few of the packers, in their western shirts and dust-covered boots, lounged against the porch rail. Quickly, Meagan scanned the group of men. She didn't see Walt.

"Here you go, young ladies." A cowboy with a rumbling voice and a curly beard reached over and swung open the screen door. Meagan pulled back, but Suzette looked up at him and dimpled.

Inside, the store closed in around her. Short aisles, holding small cans and boxes, crowded up against each other. Meagan felt as if she were squeezed into a doll's house. Even the battered metal ice cream freezer was tiny. The only regular sized thing was a revolving wire rack stuffed with new and used paperback books.

Mrs. Lindley started up one of the aisles, looking over the shelves. "Why don't you girls each pick out an ice cream?" she said, looking back over her shoulder.

Usually Mom limited their choices to frozen yogurt or juice bars, but with Mrs. Lindley they could have any kind they wanted.

Right away, Suzette asked Meagan for a fudge bar. Leaning over the cold metal case, Meagan studied her choices. Would she rather have a chocolate-coated ice cream pie or a strawberry sundae in a plastic cup with its own little wooden spoon? She looked over the possibilities with pleasure.

"I missed you this morning, girlie."

His voice was hushed, so low she couldn't tell where it came from.

Meagan froze. The edge of the ice cream chest dug into her stomach and made her feel sick. She didn't want to see Walt ever again, but she had to turn around. Facing him was better than knowing he was somewhere near, and not knowing exactly where.

He was right behind her, on the other side of the bookrack, pretending to read over the titles. Meagan watched him, but she didn't say anything. She couldn't. Her heart beat fast. Her palms felt wet and cold.

She watched as Walt turned and caught Mrs. Lindley's eye. "Howdy, Ma'am," he said, tipping his hat.

"Meegee, I don't want this. Gimme something else." A small hand tugged at Meagan's elbow. She had to turn away from the grown-ups to put the softened fudge bar back.

"Do they have the kind with three colors?"

With her head down in the icy air of the case, all Meagan could hear was the humming of the freezer's motor. She came up, a Neapolitan sandwich in one hand, just in time to hear Walt say, "You folks sure are nice to those girls. Known 'em long?"

"Why, yes." Mrs. Lindley's voice floated high and clear throughout the store. "We live in the same neighborhood back in San Luis."

"Meegee, you squished my ice cream!"

Quickly Meagan reshaped the ice cream and handed it to her sister, all the while feeling terror creeping through her. Why did Mrs. Lindley say that? Now Walt knew the town they lived in.

In a friendly, off-hand way, Walt went on. "Really, now?" That was all he had to say to keep Mrs.

Lindley talking.

"Oh, yes . . ."

Meagan gripped the edge of the freezer. Was there any way to stop Mrs. Lindley once she got going?

"As a matter of fact, we were the first two families on our road. There was nothing but artichoke fields before we built our houses side by side right there on—"

It was the only thing that Meagan could think of to do. She shoved the bookrack and sent it crashing. Down it went, banging against a display of insect repellent.

Books flew everywhere. The tower of spray cans wobbled and then slid to the floor. The wire bookrack bounced sideways against a display of bubble packs, then slowly fell, bringing flashlight batteries, diaper pins, and bootlaces with it.

There were shouts. Everybody turned to stare at the mess.

"Meegee did it!" Suzette declared amid the rubble.

No one paid any attention to her; they were too busy picking everything up.

The store man righted the wire bookrack and Meagan slipped books back in place. A cowboy from the front porch gathered up the farthest rolling cans of insect repellent. Suzette handed cards of bootlaces to Mrs. Lindley to hang back up. After most of the mess had been sorted out, Mrs. Lindley and the store owner went back to the cash register.

Meagan was on her hands and knees, picking up the last of the books, when she looked up and saw Walt watching her.

"Are you keeping your promise, little girl from San Luis?" he asked in a low voice, his eyes boring into hers.

Meagan wished that the bookrack had hit him and knocked him out cold. But she didn't dare say a word. He kept looking at her in that piercing way until she finally nodded just to get him to stop.

Then his gaze shifted from her to her sister. Suzette stood behind Mrs. Lindley, who was paying for the groceries at the tiny cash register. Flicking her bouncy red curls back from her shoulders, Suzette licked at the softened sides of her ice cream.

"You sure have one pretty little sister," Walt said to Meagan in that same low voice. "I bet you'd hate to have something happen to that little doll-baby, now wouldn't you, girlie?"

Walt didn't look at her again. Instead, he rose to his feet and left the store, smiling and tipping his hat to Mrs. Lindley as he went out the door.

7

Meagan offered to carry Mrs. Lindley's groceries for her, but the older woman just pursed her lips and picked up the bag herself. Hugging it against her broad chest, Mrs. Lindley led them across the porch, down the steps, and out from under the shade of the pines. Suzette bobbed along at her side, taking big bites of ice cream. Still shaken from her encounter with Walt, Meagan followed close behind.

If Walt knew how to find her house, she'd never be safe.

In front of her, Mrs. Lindley walked on in brisk silence. Somehow, Meagan had to keep her from telling Walt anything more. Not just for her own sake, but for Suzette's as well.

But Mrs. Lindley was obviously in no mood to talk. Meagan had never known her to be silent for so long. Finally, as they neared the stables, Mrs. Lindley spoke.

"Look, dear," she said, bending down beside Suzette. "There's a whole patch by that rock. Do you remember what those red flowers are called?"

Thoughtfully, Suzette looked them over while she licked a dribble of pink ice cream that had run down her wrist. "Finger Paint?"

Meagan knew the answer. "Paintbrush," she said.

Mrs. Lindley turned to look at her. "That's right," she said with some of her usual warmth. "Indian Paintbrush, or *Castilleja*. Such a pretty name."

Once the silence was broken, Mrs. Lindley continued to chatter to Suzette about the flowers they were passing. But Meagan fell silent again. As they started up the rise in the road, Suzette put her hand trustingly into Mrs. Lindley's.

Suzette is so little, thought Meagan. Whatever Walt meant by his threat, Meagan knew she couldn't let it happen to Suzette. Mostly, her little sister was a pest. But when Meagan thought of Walt scaring or hurting Suzette, she felt a sudden, fierce jab of anger and pain. Somehow she had to stop Walt from finding out where they lived.

By the time they were halfway up the hill, Mrs. Lindley was panting. "Want me to carry the bag?" Meagan asked again.

"I'm all right, dear. But thank you," said Mrs. Lindley. "We'll all have a little rest under the tree when we get to the top."

Mrs. Lindley smiled at her and Meagan felt relieved. If Mrs. Lindley wasn't angry after all, then maybe she'd understand. Of course Meagan couldn't tell her everything; then she'd really be in trouble with Walt. But maybe she could say just enough so that Mrs. Lindley wouldn't blow it again. She had to make Mrs. Lindley realize how important it was to not tell Walt anything more.

"At last!" puffed Mrs. Lindley when they reached the top of the rise. "Let's sit a minute," she said, setting the bag down in the shade of the twisted pine tree.

Surrounding the base of the tree were chunks of bark, shaped like jigsaw puzzle pieces. Suzette sat down among them and started trying to fit the chunks together.

"You can try all day, dear," Mrs. Lindley told her as she lowered herself onto a flat rock in the shade, "but you'll never make sense out of those."

Meagan sat on the ground next to the older woman and waited for a chance to speak.

"I just love the view from here," Mrs. Lindley said, fanning herself with one hand. "You can see so far in both directions."

Suzette had crawled around to the back of the tree, in search of a match for her puzzle piece when Meagan finally thought of a way to begin.

"Um, Mrs. Lindley?" she said, picking at the flaky, gray lichen that grew on the boulder beside her. She felt her throat tighten before she got any further.

"Yes, dear?"

"Can you keep a secret for me? I mean, there's something I don't want you to tell someone, okay?"

"Well, dear," said the older woman, pulling at the material of her blouse, as if to let in some air, "it all depends."

For a moment, Meagan was stuck. She had hoped Mrs. Lindley would say yes. "This is really important. Suzette and I could get into a lot of trouble if you told."

Mrs. Lindley drew herself up. "Oh, that," she said. "Really, your parents ought to know. I just can't imagine what got into you."

For a moment, Meagan was baffled.

"It wasn't at all the kind of thing I'd expect from you, Meagan. And that bookrack came quite close to hurting that nice young man."

"That's not what I mean," Meagan protested.

"But, my dear, I saw you push it over with my own eyes. Suzette had nothing to do with it."

Meagan felt desperate. "Mrs. Lindley," she said. "Please don't tell Walt anything more about where we live!"

The older woman stopped talking. She looked at Meagan as if she wondered if she had heard right. "Do you mean that nice cowboy? Why ever not, dear?"

This was it. Meagan felt like she was crossing a creek on a shaky log.

"Because . . . because he's after me, that's why."

Mrs. Lindley's blue curls bobbed in surprise. "Whatever gave you that idea?"

"He . . . " Meagan searched for something she could tell without breaking her promise to Walt. "I just know that he is."

"Is that all?" asked Mrs. Lindley, reaching to touch Meagan's arm. "Did he say anything, do anything to you?"

Looking into Mrs. Lindley's concerned face, Meagan wanted to tell her everything Walt had done. But she was afraid of what might happen if she did.

"Yesterday, before riding class, he held my hand."

"Oh, Meagan," said Mrs. Lindley kindly.

Meagan leaned towards her. There was relief in telling even that much.

"Oh, Meagan, dear," said Mrs. Lindley again.

Then she patted Meagan's arm briskly. "I can't imagine he meant anything by it."

Meagan felt her relief vanish. "But he did!" she insisted, pulling away.

"Oh, I believe it happened," said Mrs. Lindley. "But sometimes children misunderstand things." She shook her head as if trying to clear away a disturbing thought. "He was probably just trying to be nice to you."

That's what Meagan had thought at the time, too. But now she realized that if she'd told him to stop then, or gone to her parents, he might not have kept after her.

"Meagan, you have to be careful about what you say."

"I know that!"

"No, I don't think you do," Mrs. Lindley told her. "Talk like that can get a perfectly innocent man into a lot of trouble."

The chips of lichen fell from Meagan's hand. She'd said all she safely could. Why was Mrs. Lindley sticking up for Walt?

"Don't jump to conclusions, dear. 'Believe the best.' That's what I always try to do." The older woman stood up and brushed off the legs of her slacks as if there were dirt on them.

Disappointment stung Meagan's eyes. All the time she'd been afraid to tell, she'd never imagined that she wouldn't be believed if she did. Wordlessly, Meagan stood up.

"Oh, Suzette! Stay out of that dirt, that's a termite hill!" Mrs. Lindley seemed to have forgotten about their conversation already. "Come along, girls," she said. "And, Suzette, don't leave your ice cream wrapper behind."

They were in the shade of the forest and almost back to camp, when Mrs. Lindley spoke quietly to Meagan.

"About what happened at the store, dear. I won't mention it to your parents, if you'd like. Least said, soonest mended."

Meagan nodded in silent confusion. She wasn't so sure that Mrs. Lindley was right, but she didn't really know what else to do.

"You know, dear, it wasn't so terrible, my telling him where we're from," Mrs. Lindley continued. "Why, if anyone really wanted to find out an address, they could just look it up in the register at the lodge."

8

In the dusk, after dinner was over, Mom helped Meagan pack up the food boxes. Suzette sat at the table and pulled the ice cream wrapper out of her pocket. Spreading the soggy mess out in front of her, she started picking little dark things off it and flinging them on the ground.

"What have you got?" Meagan asked.

"Bugs," Suzette answered. "But most of them are dead."

Meagan peered at the grubby paper. It was studded with termites, some of them still struggling in the sweet glue.

"That's cruel," Meagan said. "Mom, make her let them go."

"But you told me to," Suzette protested. "You told me to feed Clifford live bugs."

Clifford. An awful realization hit Meagan.

"Suzette, where's Clifford? Did we leave him in the sand? He could suffocate in there. He could die!"

The self-righteous look on Suzette's face melted

into shock and then into a tearless wail. Without waiting for Meagan, Suzette started running for the lake trail, her chubby legs carrying her forward in an awkward trot.

Meagan caught up with her and scooped Suzette up in her arms. For a little kid, Suzette was heavy. But Meagan knew it was faster to lug her than to wait for her short legs to catch up.

"Don't die, Cliffy! Don't die!" Suzette cried over Meagan's shoulder all the way through the campgrounds and down the narrow trail to the beach.

The chill of evening met them when they broke out of the shelter of the trees and ran onto the deserted beach. Where Clifford's igloo had been, there was only a depression in the sand.

Meagan and Suzette tore open the ruined house. They raked their fingers through dry sand. On the surface the sand was cool, but underneath it still held the heat of day. The soft leaves that had lined the house crumbled in Meagan's hands. Hurrying, she turned up sticks and more dry leaves and even the pine cone dolls. But Clifford was gone.

As the pale light continued to fade, Meagan found the last trace of Clifford. A thin, waving line was pressed in the wet sand at the edge of the lake. On each side of the line, the sand pushed up in little ruffles. The tracks led down to the shallow water.

"Look, Suzette, he got free," Meagan said in relief. "He must have pushed between the sticks and climbed out through the sand. He did it all by himself."

"Cliffy's gone," wailed Suzette. She leaned out over the water and waved her grubby ice cream wrapper. "Come back, Clifford," she called. "Come back for your bugs."

A strange mixture of love and exasperation welled up in Meagan. She put her arm around her sister.

"It's okay, Suzette," she said. "Clifford can get plenty of bugs on his own. He likes them better that way."

Suzette turned to Meagan and poked her lower lip out defiantly. "Nope," she said. "Clifford likes my bugs best. He just didn't want to be all bottled up."

They were standing there, watching the blue light of evening slip into darkness, when Meagan heard footsteps crackle in the forest behind them.

A chill washed down her spine. "Quick, Suzette," she whispered, pulling her sister back from the shore.

"Quit it!" Suzette tried to yank her arm free.

Meagan heard the footsteps again. There was someone on the trail in the forest above them. Someone who walked and then stopped, as if listening for them.

"Shhhh!" Meagan warned her sister. Was it Walt? Suddenly the night seemed very dark.

Did he know she'd tried to talk to Mrs. Lindley? Was he out looking for her? "Come on," Meagan whispered, urging her sister back under the soft-leaved bushes between the beach and the forest.

Dried leaves crunched under their feet. Meagan pulled Suzette even farther back, so that a canopy of leaves and a tangle of branches stood between them and the beach. Still, through the gaps in their screen, Meagan could see big patches of white sand, glowing eerily in the dusk. It wasn't a very good hiding place.

"Quiet, now," Meagan cautioned and pulled Su-

zette down to crouch beside her where the bushes were thickest.

If only he missed them in the dark. Meagan strained to hear his approach.

The footsteps came from the beach now, hissing through the dry sand toward their hiding place. Behind them the forest loomed dense and forbidding. Meagan could almost feel the rough arms of the pine trees leaning down to engulf them. The campground seemed so far away. Why had she left camp without her parents?

Before Meagan could stop her, Suzette stood up and announced in a normal voice, "I don't like this. What do we have to hide for?"

Meagan's hand whipped out, covering her little sister's mouth. "Hush up," she whispered and then added more kindly, "it's a game." There was no point in scaring Suzette; she'd just start wailing.

With her hand pressed firmly over Suzette's mouth, Meagan listened intently to the night. The footsteps whispered past them, then stopped. Meagan wasn't sure where the person was standing or if he would be coming back. Suzette wiggled and then started whimpering against Meagan's palm. Meagan could tell how angry and scared her sister felt at being stifled.

Crouching there like a hunted mouse, Meagan hated what she was doing, hated being so scared that she shook, hated frightening her sister.

She had already been through so much. She had given up her riding lessons and the ride to Crystal Pass, taken Mrs. Lindley's scolding, and disappointed her parents. All this she had done to keep Walt's secret.

But keeping Walt's secret bottled up inside had not protected her and Suzette after all. Walt could still come after them any time he wanted. With a start, Meagan realized that the only person the secret protected was Walt.

Meagan took her hand off Suzette's mouth.

"I don't like this game," Suzette announced tearfully.

"Neither do I," said Meagan, taking her sister's moist hand in her own. "Come on, let's go home."

If they weren't going to walk straight into whoever was out there they'd have to get back through the forest. By pushing through the bushes uphill and to the right, Meagan figured, they should hit the second trail pretty fast.

Branches stuck out to trip them and prickly bushes grabbed at their clothes. The harder she struggled, the angrier Meagan became. Let Walt hear us, she thought. If he touches me or my sister I'll scream bloody murder. He can't shut us both up at once.

By the time they reached the campground, Meagan was sure of herself in the dark, and she knew just what she had to do. Suzette was right about one thing: it wasn't any fun to hide.

"Mom," Meagan said as they crashed into camp. "Mom, I've got to talk to you right *now*."

9

Mom and Daddy sat in the camp chairs, with their feet up on the stones of the fire ring. Their faces glowed in the rosy light.

"Did old Clifford make it okay?" Dad asked, turning towards Meagan and Suzette as they ran into camp.

Suzette scrambled up onto his lap and put her arms around Daddy's neck. "Cliffy wasn't in the house 'cause he ran away so we called to him but he wouldn't come back and I left my bugs for him anyhow. I don't think he liked being caught."

"I see," said Daddy, and he chuckled softly.

Planting herself next to Mom's chair, Meagan repeated, "Mom, I've got to talk to you."

Her mother looked up at her. The firelight softened Mom's strong features and made her face look almost dreamy. "Sure, honey. Just as soon as I get Suzette to bed."

But Meagan couldn't wait. Not after it had taken her so long.

"Can't Daddy do it? I need to talk with you right now. Alone."

Suzette slid off Daddy's lap and stamped her foot, raising a cloud of camp dust. "No, no, no. I want Mommy!"

"Can't it wait ten minutes?" Mom asked.

Meagan looked at her family. The courage to speak was draining from her. Suzette was about to get her way again. Meagan felt like she was shrinking back into the snail shell of fear where she had hidden most of the day.

"No," she said. "It can't wait. Something scary happened to me and I've got to talk with you, now."

Across the campfire Meagan saw Daddy's eyebrows shoot up in surprise. He hesitated a moment. "Come on, Carrot Top," he said at last, scooping Suzette up and flinging her over his shoulder. "Aren't I a good enough bed-putter for you? Wait'll you hear me sing *Baby's Boat*. I'm better than Mommy any day."

"Put me down. Put me down," shouted Suzette, but she was giggling, too.

The two of them left the circle of light and took the noise and laughter with them.

After a long silence Mom said, "What happened, honey?"

Meagan swallowed. Where should she start? The stone that had lain quietly in her throat for most of the day began to swell again until Meagan felt like she wouldn't be able to breathe, let alone speak. She looked into her mother's eyes, willing, hoping, praying for understanding. Then she sucked in her breath and said, "I think you and Daddy are wrong about promises."

"Promises?"

"I don't think you have to keep a promise, no matter what. Not if you promised to keep a secret so you could get away from someone. Not if it's a dangerous secret and you feel really bad inside and scared because you can't protect yourself and your sister."

The backs of Meagan's knees were shaking now, but she pushed on. "Sometimes people have to break promises and tell secrets because it's the right thing to do."

"Meagan?" Mom reached out to draw her near.

But Meagan stepped back. She wasn't ready to be touched. She didn't want to be comforted yet.

Mom's arm fell back into her lap; she shook her head, as if trying to rearrange her thoughts. Then she looked up at Meagan. "I think you'd better tell me exactly what happened," she said softly.

So Meagan told.

Standing there, half in and half out of the fire's warmth, she told everything. She told about Walt promising her secret lessons on Charlotte so she could learn how to go through the gates and how he met her outside the restrooms and took her down to the lake trail instead. She told about how he crushed her against his body and how scared she had been. She told about his hands inside her clothes and about how she tricked him into letting her go.

Halfway through, she began to cry. She didn't want to cry because it seemed babyish. But now that she had started talking, she wanted to tell everything that had happened. So, with her hands clenched and her eyes squeezed shut, she cried and talked at the same time.

She told her mother about the nightmare, and

about trying to stop Mrs. Lindley from telling Walt where they lived, and about Mrs. Lindley not believing her.

When she said that last part, about Mrs. Lindley acting like she'd made things up, Mom stood up and pulled Meagan into a hug. "Mrs. Lindley was wrong," Mom said hoarsely. "You were asking her for help. She should have believed you."

Then Meagan pressed her wet face against her mother's rough camp shirt and cried and cried. And the awful stone that had closed up her throat for so long turned out not to be a stone at all, but a huge bag of tears. The more she cried, the less there was in the bag, until at last she could breathe easily and quietly against her mother's chest.

"Oh, Meegee," said Mom at last, and her own voice sounded shaky. "You were so brave. I'm so glad you got away from him. And I'm so glad you told me."

The two of them stood there, holding onto each other, until Meagan felt her mother shudder. Pulling herself free from her mother's arms, Meagan asked, "Mom, what's wrong?"

Mom bit her lip, but Meagan could see the terrible look that her mother was trying to hide.

"I'm just . . . so mad," Mom said. "So angry!"

"At me?"

"Not you!" Mom's voice exploded in dismay. "At me, for not realizing something was wrong. At *him*. That Walt! He had no right to touch you like that!"

"Then why did he do it?"

"He's sick!" Mom said. "Mentally sick!" Then she shook her head and sat down on the bench of the picnic table. There was room for both of them, so

Meagan sat next to her. The bench was cold, but their bodies were still warmed by the fire.

"Some men . . . " Mom's voice choked up, then she started again. "Some people don't grow up right inside. Walt's feelings are very mixed up. A normal adult wouldn't want to touch a child that way."

"He acted like my friend, and then I felt so awful afterwards," said Meagan.

"I don't think he even thought about how you would feel," Mom told her. "He was just thinking about himself, about what he wanted to do."

"Like Suzette with Clifford?" asked Meagan. She was remembering the way Suzette rocked her captive in his bottle.

Mom laughed softly, and some of the tenseness went out of her body. "Yes, a little like that. Only Suzette learned that lesson today, thanks to you. And it's different with Walt. He's a grownup. He's responsible for what he does, no matter how he feels inside."

"I guess I shouldn't have gone off with him without asking you or Daddy," said Meagan.

"That's true," Mom said, touching Meagan's cheek with her cool fingers. "But that doesn't make what he did your fault. He knew what he did was wrong. That's why he made you promise not to tell."

Leaning her head on Mom's shoulder, Meagan looked past the fire and let out a long sigh. The secret was over; she felt relieved and tired. It had been hard work keeping Walt's secret all this time. Gently, Mom put her arm around Meagan's shoulders. Mom's hug felt good and safe.

The fire shifted. Mom cleared her throat. "Meagan, there's something you should know."

Meagan wondered what was coming.

"I know you were scared by what happened last night. Someday, when you're older and you find a partner that you love very much, like Daddy and I love each other, then touching each other's body will feel good and be a very special part of your life together. A real friend would never scare you or threaten you like Walt did. Do you understand?"

"Sure," said Meagan. "I knew all that." But it was comforting to hear Mom say it, all the same.

Wrapping her arms around herself, Meagan stared into the fire. It was weird to think about a grownup she liked being so selfish, so mean. Especially Walt, who had taught her so many good things, like how to ride Charlotte and how to handle Poco.

The fire was burning down to a tangle of red coals and gray ash. Meagan looked for the castle that she always saw in its depths. There it was, looking like a fortress in a barren landscape of burning rocks. Behind her, Daddy's voice rose from the tent. He sang *Blue Water Line*, off-key, of course, and with some of the words scrambled. But the sound was as comforting to her now as it had been when she was Suzette's age and Daddy had sung her to sleep.

"Please don't tell Daddy, okay?" Meagan said, looking up at her mother.

Mom paused before asking, "Why don't you want him to know?"

It was so hard to put the feeling into words. "Last night I would've told him, but now I feel sort of embarrassed. The worst part was feeling scared and alone. But now that you know, I'd just as soon forget all about it."

"I think we should tell Daddy and the sheriff."

"But I don't want people to know," Meagan protested. "I wish it had never happened!"

"I wish it hadn't either," said Mom.

Daddy's singing had stopped and now he stuck his head out of the tent. "Is it okay for me to come out now?" he asked. Meagan knew Daddy was trying to make a joke. But she didn't feel like laughing.

"Look," he said, more seriously. "If you two want to have a woman talk alone, I'll just go over to the Lindleys' for a while. Okay?"

Meagan nodded and Mom said, "Thanks, honey."

Once Daddy left the camp, Meagan and Mom stared into the fire in silence. The castle in the flames was even airier now. Much of the wood had burned away, and the structure that was left was built of fragile ash and glowing coals. A puff of air swirled through the camp; the fire blazed up brightly and suddenly the castle collapsed.

Mom got up and put more wood on the fire, crushing what was left of the old castle and creating a whole new landscape of sticks and logs.

"I wish I'd known earlier," Mom said, "about your wanting extra help with the gates. If you'd known about Charlotte, Walt never could have tricked you like that."

"What do you mean?" Meagan asked. When Mom turned to face her, all Meagan could see was the fire, outlining her mother with a soft orange glow.

"It's what I was trying to tell you yesterday and this morning. When we watched your lesson yesterday, Mr. Farnum told me. Charlotte has refused to go through gates ever since one hit her on the right side of her head."

"You mean it wasn't my fault?"

"No, honey. It's strange, though, because she will still go through gates if you approach them from the left. Mr. Farnum said you just can't let her see the gate out of her right eye."

The fire blared up behind Mom, bathing the whole camp in sudden red light.

"But Mom, why didn't you tell me! Why didn't you tell me right away?"

Mom jammed her hands into her pockets. "It just seemed like every time I tried to tell you, you didn't want to hear. And I guess, too, I trusted Walt to tell you, sooner or later."

The news about Charlotte made Meagan realize something else. She wasn't such a bad rider, after all. Knowing what she did now, she might well be able to open gates on horseback. "Then I could still pass the Trail Trials, couldn't I?" she asked, jumping to her feet. "I could still go on the ride with Daddy."

"I don't see why not," Mom said.

Meagan knew that if she rode in tomorrow's Trials, she'd have to see Walt. But at least Mr. Farnum was in charge of the test. It would be scary, but nothing as scary as tonight by the lake, when she couldn't even see who was there. And besides, now she had something to prove.

"I'm not going to let Walt stop me," she told her mother. "I'm not going to go around scared."

Mom put her arm around Meagan's shoulders. "I'm glad you feel brave about it, honey. Daddy and I will be right there with you."

Leaning against her mother's strong body, Meagan felt suddenly exhausted. It had been dark for so long, it must be very late, she thought.

"I want to go to bed," Meagan said. Turning away

from the fire, she pulled her towel and her pink bag down from the clothesline. At the edge of the circle of light, she hesitated.

"Do you want me to go with you?" Mom asked. "I can call Daddy to come and stay with Suzette."

Meagan shook her head. After all, she had walked to the restrooms every night that week. And she couldn't take her mother with her everywhere.

"If I see Walt I'll just yell bloody murder," she said. "And run."

Once she was beyond the campfire's glow, the forest seemed darker than ever. Something crackled in the bushes. Probably a pine cone hitting the ground, Meagan told herself, but she walked out in the middle of the road, where she'd have a running start, just in case.

It wasn't long at all before she was within the circle of yellow electric light, pushing open the heavy wooden door of the restroom.

Meagan was standing at the sink, brushing her teeth and making faces at herself in the hazy metal mirror, when a girl with black braids swung open the door behind her.

"Hi," said the girl, coming up beside Meagan. She was halfway between Meagan and Suzette in size, and Meagan thought she looked familiar. It was the girl who sat on the rail of the riding ring every day, drinking in each lesson from the sidelines.

"You're pretty good," said the girl. "At riding, I mean."

Smiling, Meagan bent to spit in the sink. She still had a lot to learn, but it felt great to be looked up to.

"I'm going to be that good, too," said the girl, flicking back her short braids. "My Mom says I can take lessons here next week."

The smile died in Meagan's heart. The girl at her side looked so eager. Meagan knew there was nothing more wonderful than finally learning to ride after you've ached for it a long time. But what if Walt tricked this girl, too?

"Listen," said Meagan quickly. "If you get Charlotte—she's the piebald mare—remember this, okay? She'll only go through gates if you approach them from the left."

The girl looked a little baffled, but she nodded eagerly. "Sure. Hey, thanks for the tip," she called as Meagan headed out the door.

Meagan ran all the way back to camp. Running, she felt stronger than ever. The night air was cool on her throat. Meagan wanted to sing or shout—do *something* at the top of her lungs.

When Meagan dashed into camp, Mom was still alone by the campfire, watching the road. Looking out for me, Meagan thought.

"I changed my mind, Mom," she called out. "I do want to tell! I want to tell Daddy and the sheriff and Mr. Farnum, too. Walt can't keep on tricking kids. It's just not fair."

Mom slipped her arm around Meagan. "You're a gutsy young woman," she told her. "Daddy and I will help you all we can."

"Where is he?" Meagan asked. "Let's tell him now."

"He's gone down to the lake. Mr. Lindley said that he was walking down there and heard some crashing and whimpering in the bushes. Daddy thought it might be a wounded animal."

Laughing, Meagan told Mom about trying to hide

Suzette in the bushes. "This time the joke's on Daddy," she said. And then she yawned.

"It's late," Mom said. "Why don't you go to bed. I'll talk things over with Daddy, and in the morning we can all plan what to do."

Meagan nodded. She was tired. Mom gave her one last, tight hug. "Goodnight, punkin'," she said.

Quietly, so as not to wake Suzette, Meagan slipped into her puffy sleeping bag. She wiggled her toes to warm up the cold nylon. Then, as the warmth of her body filled the bag, she drifted gently to sleep.

That night she dreamed of wild horses again.